# A TROVE OF VERSELETS

AVTANSH JHA

Made with ❤ on the Notion Press Platform
www.notionpress.com

# Contents

# Acknowledgements

I thank sincerely each and every person of my life who always motivated me to get going a build up my passion in form of poetry. it makes me very happy to reveal a different reality of my own world in front of everyone.

love you, mom and dad.

# Chapter1

The Olympics ‘91
When reached the final day
views and spirits said
More than these words will ever say.
The bullet when shot off the gun
The five finalist start the run
Watching stats of stadium’s wall
Was how the third one had a fall
The fifth one now stand by him near the sand
And showed the spirit by holding his hand
The second one now leaves his sprint
And gives ’em two a lovely hint
The fourth one when saw this
Had then nothing left to wish
Sniffing the choice of victory apart
He held their hands and was now their part
The first one with victory anigh
Stopped and waved his hand high
And then the race reduced to a walk
And hit the victory with a sweet knock.
The Olympics '91
When reached the final day
views and spirits said

More than these words will ever say.

# Chapter2

On a summer evening,
Old Mathew's work is done ,
He is sitting and watching,
The lost lipped sun.
Beside him comes his grand-daughter
His beloved Esther.
She sees the sun and says,
Why? Thou sit here every evening,
Old Mathew smiles and says,
For, it gives me childhood memories,
The days and nights and winters and summers,
It reminds me of my friends, family and suppers.
"Do you miss those days ? " asks she,
Replies he, " ay, but getting old is a part of life" ,
My sweet friends , family and wife,
They are whom I admire,
I was oxygen for them,
While they were the burning fire.
Quoth she, "why? A man gets old?" ,
" Is it a rule being told?",
" Nay, its what we're made for" says he,
" for living together concordantly
And to reminisce and realise

That we lived a happy life.

# Chapter3

In a foggy morning when the sun got lipped,
During our casual walk ,
An old masonry bridge was what we saw,
On which sat an old scary hawk.
The bridge without boundaries ,
Had no support,
For my friends and I,
It was tough to import.
Methought to fight it brave,
My first step gave me a jolt,
took the next step
Got balanced, by jove.
Kept doing this,
Till I reached the end,
After crossing the bridge I got to know,
Its just our preconceived fears, we need to let go

# Chapter4

Five kids playing under a tree,
One runs away,
Caught a glimpse of me
Four kids gamboling around a slide,
Two run away,
‘cause it was dusk and they were to be home,
Beside the river which was extremely wide.
Another runs away suddenly,
’Cause Darkness prevailes eerily,
Seems unperturbed though scared terribly.
The last kid too is in hurry,
Eluding my grasp warily.
And there ain’t any chance for me,
To go back home hungry.

# Chapter5

I hath love towards those pretty leaves,
Next to my depot, where I live.
That chilly time, which once I loved,
Don't know how many times I paid it a hug!
Those leaves when kissed my palms,
Can't explain the way it calms.
I hath love towards those pretty leaves,
Next to my depot, where I live.
The gloss they contain after rain
Makes me feel like I'm drab
I hath love towards those pretty leaves,
Next to my depot, where I live.
Those leaves when hewed,
Makes me feel like i'm fade.
I hath love towards those pretty leaves,
Next to my depot, where I live.

# Chapter6

Walking on the sun-bathed grass,
in search of some water in a glass.
We were a group of three,
We had some rest under a tamarid tree.

It 'as a hearty weather,
But we preferred our friendly banter
The tamarind tree served us as a shed,
And its sour tamarinds refreshed our heads.

Enjoying the tamarinds, we forgot about water.
Because at that moment, it was only our affinity that mattered!

# Chapter7

The eastbound express hits
The horns hard
On a day bitter and cold
With a girl and two men, is the story told.
The girl with luxurious comfort
Rubbing her hands in the cold weather
Enter two tall men, actually a Marshall and culprit
Were handcuffed together.
Young Mr. Oliver with his hand partner
Got some old vibes from the girl's smile
The girl, off some old meetings
Gets interested in him in just a while.
Oliver dressed smart and handsome
With his partner in dirty clothes
Seeing Oliver as a young handsome marshall
The heart of girl constantly blows.
Without any question,
Thinking of the things ahead
Oliver's partner with a sigh
Makes his seat his bed.
Reaching the station she was on to,
With a beautiful smile said she, with her heart's pop
"Aren't you young enough Oliver, for this job?"

Oliver's hand partner with a false smile says
"Dear, have you ever seen a marshall handcuffed in his right hand ways ! ".

*Mr Oliver was handcuffed on his left hand, the other guy turned out to be the marshall.

# Chapter8

Seemed to be a wavin' flag,
Few memories good, few mostly lag.
Seemed to be useless at first,
But now realised, it was a selfish thirst.
Seemed to be as sharp as a shaft,
But now can't explain how beautifully is it graphed.
This is how it has been
So far now.....
Seemed to be so blur,
But now at every instant is a joyful colour.
Seemed to be full of confusing things,
But now it has beautiful sky and joyful wings.
Seemed to be has hard as a rock,
But now those happy vibes give a shock.
This is how it has been
So far now......
Seemed to be a fake sadness-reflecting mirror,
Now there's no place for sorrow here.
Seemed to be a bad dream,
But now only happiness and joy scream.
Seemed to be a fake sinless nerd,
But now it flies high like a beautiful bird.

This is how it has been
So far now.....

# Chapter9

Methought I'm wrong today,
Like all of 'em I have seen.
But now I want my words to be true,
'cause a lie it has always been.
When the truth came outta me,
Everything was true.
Still majority didnot believe,
But yeah there were few.
If not this day,
Such words are,
It was for them to say,
Everything was far.
'em worded me weird,
When being lone wolf I sat,
Yes I know I was,
Weird like a three cornered hat.

# Chapter10

From years and months and months and years
Which they never did get
Is never ,never, NEVER let them
Near your television set.
They sit and stare and stare and sit
And the drama hitting them with stick
And they shout out loud
And watch 'till their eyes pop out.
Those days, how they used to entertain ?
I'll answer that loud and clear
They'd read and read and then proceed
Comics and books of Mr Bean and Seed
What when this monster was not invented?
They'd read and read and stay contented !
Instead of that television screen
When gets free the hall
Then with lovely books
Install a lovely bookshelf on the wall.
And once they have nil to do
They'd start reading a sheet
And then thee see ,they shalt see
The difference of the useless screen.

Then later each and every kid,
Will love you more for what you did.

# Chapter11

Winter sirens building up the news,
Said "grenades and deaths did fall".
With destructions and damages and deaths,
Started the dangerous civil war.
With birds that fly,
Above the land so high,
How strange was it for them?
When they knew the death anigh.
The old man at church,
With all his hopes alive,
But the war did say so?
Which made dead husbands, children and wives.
With praising of wining side,
The winter turned out cold.
They didnt know after this victory,
Their happiness was sold.
Their guns held in death-still hands,
Was proof of human sin.
They did not die from the cold without,
They died from the cold within.

# Chapter12

Yours truly and his friends,
Went into a town.
While we facin‘ down,
Appears to be a forsaken town.
Struggling and chasing the taxi-cab,
He asked the spot.
We five cried prisoner's land,
He alone cried "i'm off".
After few hours, we set in the town,
Standing in front of a petrifying door.
Three men arrive saying-
"isn't this much satisfying? Or you want more".
Holy! Two got caught persist were three,
Then i woke up.
I realised,
It was a shitty dream.

# Chapter13

## THE SCADMAR DAY

List of characters :

JIMMY

PIXIE

TRENT

LIESEL

# Chapter14

SCENE 1 FROM ST. PETERSBURG, HIMMEL.

PIXIE- AHH! I'M BORED. CAN'T WE HAVE AN ADVENTUROUS DAY TOMORROW?

JIMMI- YES, WE CAN. LET'S POUR ONTO SCADMAR TOMORROW! ITS ONE OF THE MOST SPOOKY PLACES HERE.

LIESEL- (with a chaotic smile) AYY. NO WAY. I THINK YOU FORGOT TO CHECK THE NEWS THAT ARRIVED YESTERDAY. "a girl went to Scadmar alone and is now lost."

TRENT- OH YEAH! THAT'S GREAT. WE'LL HAVE SOME ADVENTUROUS HOURS AND WE'LL FIND THAT GIRL TOO AND WE WILL WIN $2400 FROM THE POLICE STATION. THAT'S AWESOME.

LIESEL- THAT WAS'NT FUNNY AT ALL.

PIXIE- OH COME ON. DON'T BE SILLY MY GIRL. WE'LL HAVE A GREAT DAY TOMORROW.

LIESEL- WELL, ALRIGHT. DONE. BUT WE WON'T STAY FOR MORE THAN AN HOUR THERE.

JIMMY- OK. SO TOMORROW AT 9 REPORT TO MY FARMHOUSE. AND ITS ABOUT TO TURN 11. SO BETTER HAVE SOME SLEEP. GOOD NIGHT GUYS.

LIESEL & PIXIE- GOOD NIGHT.

**JIMMY- HAHA. LOOK! TRENT IS ALREADY DREAMING.**

**They went home.**

# Chapter15

SCENE 2 FROM JIMMY'S FARM HOUSE , HIMMEL.

TRENT- ARE WE READY?

JIMMY- PAY ME 2 MINUTES. I DON'T KNOW WHAT'S WRONG WITH MY CAR.

PIXIE- GUYS, I'M GETTING SOME SCARY VIBES. CAN'T WE FORGET THIS PLAN AND HAVE SOME DELICIOUS ITEMS AT THE NEW BAR NEXT TO MY HOUSE? PLEASE.

LIESEL- AH. DON'T START AGAIN.

JIMMY- HERE WE GO.

They adjust themselves in Jimmy's car.

TRENT- DO YOU KNOW WHICH WAY WE NEED TO GO?

JIMMY- ACCORDING TO MY MAP, HARDLY 5 HOURS SHOULD BE TAKEN TO REACH OUR DESTINATION.

SO, BETTER ENJOY THE RIDE!

6 hours later.

JIMMY- FINALLY.

PIXIE- I'M HAPPY THAT WE'RE ALIVE. SO? WHAT'S THE NEXT PLAN?

TRENT- DON'T MAKE US DROP YOU HERE.

LIESEL- OH, COME ON GUYS. STOP FIGHTING.

**LET'S CAPTURE THIS MOMENT IN OUR HEARTS.**

**They foot-in into the town**

**TRENT- THERE'S NOT A SINGLE MAN HERE? WHAT'S THE REASON BEHIND THAT?**

**PIXIE- AFTER 4 IN THE EVENING, YOU'LL NEVER SEE ANYONE HERE. THEY'RE HOME. AND I THINK WE SHOULD STAY IN THE CAR SITTING THE SAME AS WE'RE NOW TO ESCAPE THE NIGHT.**

**JIMMY- YES.**

**LIESEL- TOMORROW WE'LL LEAVE AT 9. OK? AFTER HAVING SOME BREAKFAST.**

**PIXIE- 'RE YA CRAZY? WE'LL LEAVE AS SOON AS POSSIBLE.**

**Slowly-slowly while talking they all fell asleep.**

**-exeunt**

# Chapter16

SCENE 3 FROM SCADMAR,

PIXIE - GUYS? WHERE 'RE YA'LL? IF THIS IS A STUPID PLAN TO SCARE ME THEN PLEASE STOP!

She screams in a chaotic manner for 15 minutes.

PIXIE- AH! STUPID ME! THEY MUST BE IN A RESTAURANT. I THINK I SHOULD WAIT.

40 mins passed.

PIXIE- AY. GUYS!! WHERE YA'RE?

She fell on her seat and woke up. But, suddenly something unexpected happens

PIXIE- HUH? MY HOME? HOW'S THAT EVEN POSSIBLE.

JIMMY (knocks her door)- PIX, ARE YA READY?

PIXIE- YES READY AND ALREADY HAD A NICE ADVENTUROUSE MINUTES OF THOUGHTS AND WILL NEVER GET BORED AGAIN.

JIMMY – HUH? I DON'T GET IT.

PIXIE- YOU WON'T.

Pixie wakes up and realizes that she experienced some maniac thoughts while she was asleep all along.

-exeunt

Had a great time writing this book, I hope going through this book brought you happiness. Though I'm just 16, I had no idea of a level greatness of printing books so I did as my level made me do.

I tried my level best to reach the expectations.

sayonara.

9 798889 757979

Printed by Libri Plureos GmbH in Hamburg, Germany